To: Theo

From: JH mimi
papa

How to Catch a Dinosaur

From the *New York Times*
Bestselling Author and Illustrator
Adam Wallace & Andy Elkerton

sourcebooks
wonderland

Tomorrow's the big science fair!

I've never won before.

But this year I know I cannot lose

because I'm catching a **Dinosaur**!

The crocs and sharks we know today
were here when the dinosaurs ruled.
It makes no sense ALL dinos are gone.
On this point, I cannot be fooled.

MEGALODON

Dino

We head straight to our local **park**
to pick up some kind of trail.
Wait! What's that thing over there?
YES! I think it's a DINOSAUR TAIL!

The dino is more bird than reptile;

we learned in science class that's true.

And this one left something behind—

I've got our first dinosaur clue!

Looks like we've got a plant eater.

The venus flytrap had no chance.

She danced right by our **volcano**

and knew the exit at first glance.

This **CLEVER GIRL** runs fast as the wind
and dodged our trap in a hurry.
But we've got more in store for her,
so this is no time to worry.

Was she watching when I tested each trap
with my action figures and toy bricks?
It's like she knows how each **trap** works...
Can it be she's onto my tricks?

Well that didn't go according to plan.

She slipped right past our noses

and if that isn't bad enough,

I ruined Mom's prize-winning ROSES.

We made a prehistoric playground
and with lots of friends to play,

our dino won't be able to resist.

This time she won't get away!

Tall enough to stop a GiANT,

our trap had pulleys, ropes, and decks.

But this dino smashed it all to pieces.

She should be called T. *wrecks!*

My mom is an engineer,

so I've learned a trick or three.

Our **Robo Hugger 9000**™

won't let our dino go free!

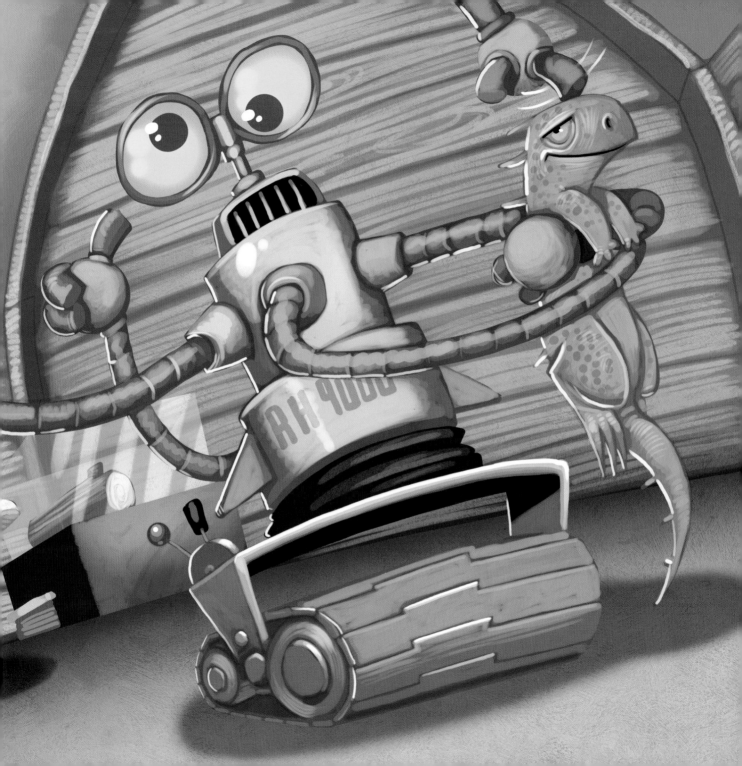

That clever dino tricked our **ROBOT**
by dressing like a bird!
If I don't catch the dinosaur soon,
I'll be lucky to come in third!

We didn't catch the **Dinosaur**.

I don't know what to do!

But my friends remind me we still have

a science fair entry or two...

FAIR

1st Prize

Better luck next time!

Copyright © 2019 by Sourcebooks, Inc.
Text by Adam Wallace
Illustrations by Andy Elkerton
Cover and internal design © 2019 by Sourcebooks, Inc.

Sourcebooks and the colophon are registered trademarks of Sourcebooks, Inc.

The art was first sketched, then painted digitally with brushes designed by the artist.

Published by Sourcebooks Wonderland, an imprint of Sourcebooks Kids
P.O. Box 4410, Naperville, Illinois 60567-4410
(630) 961-3900
sourcebookskids.com

Library of Congress Cataloging-in-Publication Data is on file with the publisher.

Source of Production: Shenzhen Wing King Tong Paper Products Co. Ltd.,
Shenzhen, Guangdong Province, China
Date of Production: April 2022
Run Number: 5025798

Printed and bound in China.

WKT 13